The Missing Rock Star Caper

The Missing Rock Star Caper

BY R. PARKER McVEY

Illustrations by Jackie Rogers

TROLL ASSOCIATES

Library of Congress Cataloging in Publication Data

McVey, R. Parker.
    The missing rock star caper.

    (Solve-it-yourself)
    Summary: The reader follows clues and directs the
course of the investigation into the mysterious disappearance of a famous rock star.
        1. Children's stories, American.   2. Plot-your-own
stories.   [1. Mystery and detective stories.
2. Plot-your-own stories]   I. Rogers, Jackie, ill.
II. Title.   III. Series.
PZ7.M47884Mi   1985   [Fic]   84-8721
    ISBN 0-8167-0398-1 (lib. bdg.)
    ISBN 0-8167-0399-X (pbk.)

10   9   8   7   6   5   4   3   2   1

Warning!

In this story, *you* are the detective! *You* must find the clues, follow the leads, and try to solve the mystery.

But do not read this book from beginning to end. Start on page 1, and keep reading till you come to a choice. After that, the story is up to you. Your decisions will take you from page to page.

Think carefully before you decide. Some choices will lead you to further clues. But other choices may bring about a quick end to your investigation—and to you!

Whatever happens, you can always go back to the beginning and start again. Best of luck in your investigation.

YOU

LIEUTENANT TRAPP

DEBBI LAMBSWOOD

VINCENT CARY,

BILL BENTWICK

BJORN STORM

SISSY WHITE

RAYMOND DESMO
M.D.

BOSTON BORZOI

PAPPY

You awaken to the ringing of your phone. From your pillow, you glance over at the digital clock that sits on your night table. It is 6:07 A.M.

When the phone rings for the fifth time, you pull yourself from the covers and stumble out into the hallway.

"Hello," you say in a sleepy voice.

"Hi, it's me," a pleasant voice says on the other end of the line.

You recognize the voice of your longtime family friend Debbi Lambswood. Debbi is captain of the high-school cheerleaders and part-time nurse's aide at Oak Hills Memorial Hospital.

"Hi, Debbi," you say. "It's awfully early, isn't it?"

"I know. I'm sorry," she says. "But I'm at the hospital and something's happened. I think you should come down here."

"What's up?"

"A patient is missing," she says. "Bjorn Storm, the rock-and-roll star. He was injured in a fall at yesterday's concert. I was on duty when they brought him to the emergency room last night."

You figure Debbi must be very tired after being up all night. "Can you tell me what happened?" you ask.

"All I know is that first his nurse was called away for a few minutes. Then there was a commotion at the other end of the corridor. When the nurse finally got back to Bjorn Storm's room, he had vanished."

"Hmmm," you say. "Are the police there?"

"Yes, Lieutenant Trapp of the Oak Hills police department is here."

"Oh, brother," you say. "Trapp gets nervous when I'm around." The lieutenant has yet to learn to appreciate your skills as an amateur detective.

"Please come," Debbi says. "There's something strange going on here, and I don't think that Trapp is aware of it. I think that some members of the hospital staff are involved, and . . ."

Suddenly Debbi stops talking, and you hear what sounds like a struggle. Then someone at the other end hangs up the phone with a sharp click.

If Debbi is in trouble, you think, I don't have any choice but to get involved in this case.

If you decide to go to the hospital to investigate, turn to page 5.

If you decide to go first to the auditorium where Bjorn Storm's concert was held, turn to page 10.

If you decide to go to the hospital, but in a disguise, turn to page 7.

4

You rush out to Lieutenant Trapp in the emergency-room area. Going right up to him, you ask him to step aside with you for a minute.

"Listen to this," you say, taking out your tape recorder.

Trapp listens to your recording of Bentwick's end of the conversation with Boston Borzoi.

"Where can I find this guy?" Trapp asks.

You tell him, and Trapp is off like a grizzly bear. He arrests Bentwick in the corridor outside his office. Within minutes, Bentwick tells all, hoping to save his own neck.

Over the next thirty minutes, Boston Borzoi is also arrested, and Bjorn Storm and Debbi Lambswood are found and set free.

You have done quite a job. Lieutenant Trapp offers to take you out to dinner to show his appreciation.

THE END

When you arrive at the hospital, the first thing you see is an exhausted-looking Lieutenant Trapp. He is standing near the entrance to the emergency-room waiting area, talking to an older doctor. Later you will find out from a nurse that the older doctor is in fact the hospital chief of staff, Dr. Raymond Desmond.

You know that your only chance of solving this case depends on how well you manage to stay out of Lieutenant Trapp's way. Trapp is a good detective, but he is protective of whatever he considers to be his turf. And he considers almost *everything* his turf.

By making friendly conversation with hospital staffers, you learn that the nurse who was assigned to Bjorn Storm was Sissy White. Sissy, you learn, is now sleeping in the nurses' lounge. She had been too nervous, and too curious about the fate of her famous patient, to go home at the end of her shift.

You figure that Sissy will be one of the most important people with whom you must talk. You decide to wait awhile, then question her.

In the meantime, you settle into a chair in the emergency-room waiting area. Taking out your notebook, you write down "Sissy White, Registered Nurse, assigned to monitor B. Storm's condition, off duty at 11:30 P.M. last night (Friday). Stayed over in hospital. Will question."

As you write, you look up from your pad as a man walks past. You catch only the man's profile for a few seconds, then the back of his head. You would know the face anywhere. Boston Borzoi is a notorious underworld figure. And it was alleged in the newspapers that he is moving his crime organization into the lucrative business of promoting rock concerts.

You are tired of sitting still. It's time to get moving.

If you decide that it's okay to wake up Sissy White and question her, turn to page 12.

If you decide to find out what Borzoi is doing here, turn to page 23.

from page 3

You remember that last summer a friend of yours, Bobby Lake, worked at the hospital as a volunteer. You know that he still has the white uniform that he wore on the job.

When you call Bobby on the phone, he agrees to lend you his old uniform. Before you leave home, you rummage through your disguise closet and find a pair of eyeglasses with plain glass lenses. You also take your micro-cassette recorder, and a small plastic flower that you will wear in a buttonhole. The miniature microphone from the tape recorder fits nicely into the back of the flower.

After stopping at Bobby Lake's house and changing into his uniform, you head right to the hospital. Your tape recorder is tucked into your belt and covered with your shirt. The microphone wire runs up to the top button of the shirt, where it is attached to the tiny microphone in the flower. You are ready for action.

Your friend Debbi Lambswood is in danger. To rescue her, you will have to crack the whole case. That means finding Bjorn Storm, the missing rock star.

At the hospital, you take Bobby Lake's advice and look around for a wheelchair that is not in use.

"Just find one and push it around," Bobby told you. "Nobody will suspect that you're not on the staff."

You go to the hospital, find a wheelchair, and begin your investigation. On the surface, the hospital and staff seem to be functioning normally. There's some confusion down in the emergency-room area, but that's because Lieutenant Trapp has set up shop down there. He is questioning members of the hospital staff.

Taking advantage of your semi-official status, you visit each of the four floors of the hospital and strike casual conversations as you go. You learn only two things of any interest.

One: a young x-ray technician, Bill Bentwick, was acting strangely just prior to and after the disappearance of Storm. Two: Boston Borzoi, a known underworld leader, was seen around the hospital earlier this morning. One nurse who saw Borzoi reported that he took the stairs to the hospital's basement.

If you decide to track down Bill Bentwick, turn to page 66.

If you decide to check the hospital's basement for the notorious Boston Borzoi, turn to page 18.

You don't think it was a coincidence that Bjorn Storm had an "accident" and was then kidnapped. The two events must be connected.

You go to the Oak Hills High School auditorium where Storm's concert was held. Debbi Lambswood told you that the rock star had fallen from the front of the stage.

Luckily the auditorium is open. You won't have to climb in through a window. When you get inside, you find that the cleaning crew has not yet been there.

Checking the stage, you find the boards broken through right at front and center. You assume that this is where Storm took his fall.

On closer inspection, you discover that the boards have been sawed almost all the way through! Whoever did this was aware of Storm's habit of dancing at the very edge of the stage during a performance.

The police, you assume, haven't been here yet. But you are sure that Lieutenant Trapp soon will be. You must try to find out who sawed the board.

Turn to page 16.

from page 6

If you had a motto, it would probably be "one step at a time." Sissy White might tell you something that will explain Boston Borzoi's presence in the hospital.

You knock on the door marked "Nurses' Lounge." A groggy voice from inside tells you to enter.

Inside, sitting up on a leather couch, is a pretty nurse wearing a wrinkled uniform.

"Miss White?" you ask.

"Yes," she says, rubbing her eyes.

"Early this morning, my friend Debbi Lambswood called me from the hospital. She wanted to tell me something about the disappearance of Bjorn Storm. She said there was something strange going on here. But before she had a chance to finish what she was saying, someone grabbed the phone. I have no idea where she is now."

"Debbi was on duty with me last night," Sissy White says. "She stayed here in the lounge, and we talked about the whole thing until it got very late."

"Do you have any idea what she might have meant by 'something strange'?"

"Yes and no," the nurse says. "When Bjorn Storm disappeared, there was a lot of commotion on our floor. While it was going on, both Debbi and I noticed that some members of the hospital staff behaved strangely. But we couldn't put a finger on it."

"Could you give me an example?"

"Well," she says, "Bill Bentwick, our new x-ray technician, just stood against a wall and watched what was going on. But just before Storm had disappeared, Bentwick was involved in a commotion down the corridor from Storm's room. It struck me, and Debbi, that he looked almost pleased with himself."

Writing all this down in your notebook, you ask, "Do you know what the commotion was about?"

"Yes," says Sissy. "Bill was arguing loudly with Pappy, one of our custodians, about some papers that were missing from Bill's office. He accused Pappy of having removed them. And Pappy said he never touched anything that wasn't in the wastebasket."

"Then what happened?"

"Several members of the staff stepped in to separate the two of them. I was on my way back to Storm's room when I stopped and listened to the argument. When it was over, I went back, and Storm was gone."

"Interesting," you say. "Who called you away from your post in Bjorn Storm's room?"

"That was Dr. Cary. He had me paged. He was visiting one of his patients, and said that he wanted to discuss something with me. But when I got to the other patient's room, there was only a note there that said everything was okay."

"Do you still have that note?" you ask.

"Yes," she says, reaching into the pocket of her uniform.

You take the note and look at it.

"Do you mind if I keep this?" you ask.

"No," Sissy White says. "Hold on to it if you think it can help."

"Miss White," you begin to say.

"Please call me Sissy," she says.

"Sissy," you say, "since Debbi has already disappeared, I hope you'll be very careful. Do you have a friend that you can stay with until this blows over?"

"Yes, I do. This is getting scary."

"I agree," you say.

After taking a telephone number where Sissy can be reached, you leave the nurses' lounge. The trail, you think, is not yet hot, but it's not cold either.

If you decide to find Pappy and question him, turn to page 78.

If you decide to check up on Bill Bentwick, turn to page 20.

from page 10

As you exit the auditorium, two members of the cleaning staff are just about to enter. You know both—their names are Ed and Charlie.

"Big mess in there," you say.

"We know," Ed says. "We saw it last night. We wanted to get to it right after the concert, but there was too much commotion after the rock star's accident."

"Was either of you around before the concert?" you ask.

"Charlie was," says Ed.

"I was on duty while they were setting up their equipment," Charlie says.

"Did you see anyone doing anything to the front of the stage?" you ask.

Charlie pauses to think.

"No, I didn't see anything like that," he says.

"Are you sure?" you ask. "Did anything happen that disturbed you or seemed to be unusual?"

"Hmmm," Charlie says. "There was one thing. I was supposed to be the first one here. It was my job to let in the set-up crew. But just as I got here, a guy walked out of the auditorium. He was carrying a tool box. He was kind of tall and thin. And he had brown hair."

"Did you say anything to him?" you ask.

"I asked him who he was. He just said 'electrician,' and kept walking. He was dressed funny for an electrician, though."

"How so?" you ask.

"He was wearing a white uniform, like he worked in a restaurant," Charlie says.

"Or maybe a hospital?" you ask.

"I guess so. He could have worked in a hospital," Charlie says.

"Thanks. You've both been a big help," you say.

If you decide to go right to the hospital, turn to page 24.

If you decide to talk to the other members of Bjorn Storm's band, turn to page 74.

On your way to the basement stairs, a doctor stops you.

"Come with me, please," she says.

"I can't. I'm on my way . . ." you start to say, but the doctor interrupts you.

"Nonsense," she says. "I need your help and your wheelchair. Now come with me."

You follow her into the emergency-room area. She leads you to where a boy with a cane is standing. You assist the boy into the wheelchair. Then the doctor turns to you.

"This is Jimmy Symonton," she says. "You are assigned to look after him until his tests are completed," she says.

Again, you try to come up with an excuse, but the doctor won't listen. You have been left in charge of Jimmy Symonton. And while you have pleasant conversations with the boy as you take him from one laboratory to the next, your investigation never gets off the ground.

THE END

20

from page 15

You are eager to find out more about this Mr. Bentwick. You head out to the information desk in the emergency-room waiting area. In the hospital directory, you look up the floor and room number of Bill Bentwick's office. The office is right on the main floor.

As you leave the waiting area, you catch the eye of Lieutenant Trapp. He studies you coolly. That kind of look is like a spoken warning: "Stay out of this." You can see that Trapp doesn't want you interfering with his official investigation.

Bentwick's office is halfway down the corridor. You peek inside and see a man in his mid-twenties sitting with his feet up on a desk.

He sees you, too.

"What can I do for you?" he asks.

"Mr. Bentwick?"

"Yes," he says, studying you. "Call me Bill."

"I'm a friend of Debbi Lambswood's," you say. You describe the telephone call you received from Debbi early this morning, and how someone grabbed the phone from her.

"And have you spoken to her since?" Bentwick asks.

"No. I can't locate her."

Bentwick looks over your shoulder and says, "How about you, Boston, have you seen that pretty nurse's aide?"

You turn to face Boston Borzoi, who has quietly entered the office. He closes the door behind him.

"Yeah," Borzoi says, "I've seen her. What's the big deal?"

"This friend of hers thinks she's missing," Bentwick says.

"She's not missing at all. I saw her just a few minutes ago. Want me to take you to her?" Borzoi asks you.

You are in trouble, and you know it. Both men are toying with you. You feel that a trap is about to spring —on you.

"No, that's okay," you say, moving toward the door. "I'll take your word for it. Just so long as someone has seen her and talked to her. Thanks a lot."

You've bluffed them right back. Your little speech gives you just enough time to yank the door open and run. You head straight for the emergency-room waiting area. All you want to do is get to Lieutenant Trapp.

The lieutenant is still in the waiting area, talking to a uniformed police officer.

Quickly, you tell Trapp about Debbi's call and her disappearance. Then you tell how Borzoi just told you he could take you to Debbi.

"What?" Trapp says, raising his voice. "Boston Borzoi is in this hospital?"

"Yes, sir," you say.

"Where?"

You tell Trapp where you just left Borzoi and Bentwick.

Now you learn just how good a police officer Lieutenant Trapp is. He rounds up Borzoi and Bentwick and gets them to confess.

The two men reveal where they've hidden both Debbi Lambswood and Bjorn Storm. They also inform on two other members of the hospital's staff who were involved.

You've solved the missing rock star caper. Debbi, Bjorn Storm, and all the doctors and nurses thank you. Even Lieutenant Trapp has to admit it—you're a fine detective.

THE END

from page 6

You turn and follow Borzoi through a set of double doors marked "Authorized Personnel Only." You don't usually disobey rules, but in this case you feel obliged to ignore the sign.

Keeping your distance, you watch Borzoi enter the administrative offices. You keep walking past the door. The nameplate outside reads "Raymond Desmond, M.D., Chief of Staff."

You are puzzled. Why would a notorious underworld figure just walk into the office of the hospital's top administrator?

You wait near the other end of the hall, pretending to read notices on a bulletin board. You see the doctor you saw talking to Lieutenant Trapp walk through the double doors and enter Desmond's office. You assume that this must be Dr. Desmond himself.

If you take the direct approach and go into the office to question both men, turn to page 68.

If you decide to wait for one or both of the men to come out of the office, turn to page 81.

from page 17

When you get to the hospital, the first thing you notice is the imposing figure of Lieutenant Trapp. He is talking to a nurse.

You think it's a good idea to avoid crossing over into Trapp's territory. You have two leads that you can follow.

If you decide to try to find Debbi Lambswood, turn to page 30.

If you decide to look for the hospital worker who was seen in the high-school auditorium, turn to page 88.

from page 80

You do not have a good feeling about going to see Bill Bentwick. Pappy's negative opinion of the new x-ray technician seems to be genuine.

You look up Bentwick's name in the hospital directory. His office is located in a wing just off the emergency-room area.

Just as you reach Bentwick's office, a stairway door opens at the end of the hall. Boston Borzoi and a member of the hospital staff step into the corridor. They are laughing.

You put on your most innocent expression, and continue walking in their direction. As you pass them, they barely notice you. But you see the name tag worn by the hospital staffer on his breast pocket: "W. Bentwick."

If you decide to follow them, turn to page 87.

If you decide to stop and ask them questions, turn to page 97.

Moving back toward Bentwick's office, you see that there is no one in the office next to his. You scoot inside with your wheelchair. And you're in luck! There's an air vent at the base of the wall between the two offices.

You get down on your knees and put your ear to the vent.

"The point I'm trying to make, Boston, is that it's all around the hospital that the Lambswood girl is missing," you hear Bentwick say to someone on the phone—someone named "Boston."

Bentwick is connected with Boston Borzoi, the underworld leader!

You quickly turn on your tape recorder, and hold your artificial flower up to the vent.

"I heard it from one of those volunteer kids who push wheelchairs around. The kid specifically mentioned that a nurse's aide was missing," Bentwick says.

Bentwick is silent for a few seconds as he listens to Borzoi's reaction.

"All right, Boston," he says. "You're right. I'll just continue to play it the same. I got you. By the way, how's the rock star doing?"

Bentwick is silent for a moment, then he laughs. "Great, Boston. Okay. I'll stop up there in a while. 'Bye," Bentwick says, and hangs up the phone.

If you wait for Bentwick to lead you to Boston Borzoi, turn to page 31.

If you turn all of your evidence over to Lieutenant Trapp right now, turn to page 4.

from page 80

Entering the back of the hospital, you find a stairway that leads downstairs. When you get to the basement, you have no idea where the so-called "hidden rooms" might be. You turn to the right and begin to wander through a maze of passageways. Along the way, you pass several doors with signs that read. "Storage Room," all of which are securely locked.

As you walk slowly along, you hear footsteps moving in your direction. Quickly you duck behind some cartons. As the footsteps approach, you hear parts of a conversation.

"That ought to take care of that problem," one voice says, as two men pass your hiding place.

"Pretty clever of you, Billy boy," the other voice replies.

You catch only a glimpse of the two men. But it is enough to see that one of them is Boston Borzoi. You guess that the other man, "Billy," is none other than Bill Bentwick, the x-ray technician.

If you decide to continue down the passageway, away from the two men, turn to page 35.

If you decide to follow Bill Bentwick and Boston Borzoi, turn to page 87.

from page 24

Finding Debbi Lambswood is now at the top of your list. Not only is her safety important to you, but she probably has information that could help you crack this case.

By asking around at different nurses' stations, you learn that Debbi has not been seen today at all. One nurse, Sissy White, claimed that Debbi left the hospital after her shift last night. But you know that Debbi was here at least until she called you this morning.

Sissy White, you think, is either mistaken or lying.

You also ask if there is anyone on the hospital staff who fits the description of the "electrician" at the high-school auditorium.

One young nurse tells you: "That sounds like Billy Bentwick from X-ray."

Sissy White, when given the description, just shrugs nervously.

You have two good leads.

If you decide to find out more about Sissy White, turn to page 40.

If you decide to investigate Bill Bentwick, turn to page 117.

from page 28

You've got to give Bentwick plenty of room to move. He's already seen you once. If he thinks you're watching him, your cover will be blown.

You push the wheelchair down to the far end of the corridor. Then you position yourself near a shorter corridor that you can duck down if Bentwick comes in your direction.

After several minutes, Bentwick leaves his office and heads back toward the emergency-room area. You follow with the wheelchair.

You get to the emergency-room area just in time to see Bentwick leave through the double doors on the opposite side. You push the wheelchair through the doors after him.

Some fifty feet away, Bentwick waits for an elevator. You can't go near him, or you'll make him suspicious. But what if you seem to be going about your business?

Quickly, you turn around and push the chair back through the doors into the emergency-room area. Sitting in the waiting area is a young boy with his arm in a cast.

"Want to go for a ride?" you ask him.

"Sure," he says. He hops into the chair.

Just be very quiet when we get into the elevator," you tell him.

You turn around, go back through the doors, and head for the elevators. Bentwick is just getting aboard.

The door to the elevator is closing when you get there, but you hit the call button and the door reopens.

You squeeze your occupied wheelchair into the crowded elevator. Bentwick looks at you suspiciously. But you know that having a "real" patient in your chair makes you practically immune from suspicion.

Other people get off at the second and third floors, but not Bentwick. That means he's going to the fourth, the top, floor.

You get off first and then wait, pretending to attend to your patient. Bentwick passes you and turns down the corridor. He looks back over his shoulder at you, but you pretend not to notice.

Bentwick knocks on the door of the last room on the right. Someone opens it from within, and Bentwick goes inside.

If you decide to find out what's going on in that room, turn to page 56.

If you decide to go to Lieutenant Trapp, turn to page 43.

from page 81

You know where to find Dr. Desmond when you need to speak with him. But Borzoi could disappear if you don't keep an eye on him.

Just as you get through the double doors, you see that Borzoi has already passed through the emergency-room waiting area. He enters a corridor that runs the length of the other wing of the hospital.

You walk quickly after him, just in time to see Borzoi pass through a door to the stairway. Approaching the door, you peek through its small window. Borzoi is heading for the basement. You count to ten—rushing to finish a little more quickly than you should—and follow Borzoi down the stairs.

At the bottom of the stairs, you find a dimly lit passageway with several doors on each side. Except for the sound of footsteps, the basement is silent. Assuming the footsteps belong to Borzoi, you head in their direction.

Suddenly you hear two men talking right around the next turn. You freeze.

"She's awfully pretty, isn't she?" you hear one man say.

"Too bad nobody will ever see her again," says the other. Both men chuckle.

Then you hear the sound of digging, and the sound of metal scraping against stone.

Your heart is pounding. They must have Debbi, and they are burying her alive!

If you charge around the corner to confront the men, turn to page 39.

If you duck out of the way and wait for the men to finish and leave, turn to page 49.

from page 29

You head down the basement passageway in the direction from which Bentwick and Borzoi just came. Your instinct tells you that an important link in the case is down here somewhere. You just have to find it.

But as the passageway turns left, you come to a dead end—a cinder-block wall.

"Where," you wonder, "could those two have come from?"

You must think for a moment. Putting your hand against the wall, you lean against it while you ponder your next move.

Your fingertips rest against something wet. You turn and push your index finger into the mortar between two cinder blocks.

The cement is fresh! With care you trace the dimensions of the blocks that are held by wet mortar. These include an area two blocks wide and six blocks high, more than enough room for a person to fit through.

Pappy told you that Bill Bentwick probably knows about the existence of hidden rooms. Could one of those rooms lie behind this wall? Bentwick, you think, may have carefully taken apart the wall. Then, after he had hidden some person or thing inside, he put fresh cement on the blocks and resealed the room.

You must get inside the hidden room immediately.

Searching around for something with which to dig out the cement and loosen the blocks, you find a screwdriver sitting on top of an old crate. In no time, you have one block loose. You gently pry it until you can grip it on both sides. Then you slowly pull out the block. Someone is inside!

"Debbi!" you exclaim, as your eyes meet those of your good friend. Bentwick has left her sealed in there, bound and gagged.

Working even faster, you pull out the rest of the freshly mortared blocks. You enter the room and untie Debbi Lambswood. She is weak and upset. She didn't think she would ever be found.

"Who did this to you?" you ask.

"Two men," she answers. "They grabbed the phone while I was talking to you. One of them was a hospital worker. I saw his name tag—W. Bentwick. The other man was older and wore a suit. I've seen his face before but I can't remember where."

That's Boston Borzoi, you think.

"Can you tell me if anyone else is involved besides these two?" you ask.

"I don't know for sure," Debbi says, trying to calm down, "but they kept referring to the 'Doc,' as if a doctor was involved."

"Earlier," you say, "I saw Borzoi, the older man, talking to"—you pause to check your notebook—"Dr. Vincent Cary, a surgeon."

"Dr. Cary is a good friend of mine," Debbi says. "He would never be involved in something like this."

"Can you say that for sure?" you ask.

"Well . . ." Debbi falters. "I guess not, but he's always seemed so nice. Anyway, what would he stand to gain?"

"That's the problem with this entire case," you say. "What has anyone to gain? What could be a possible motive?"

While you bring Debbi upstairs and get her a taxi to take her home, you mull over what you should do next.

If you decide to search for a motive, turn to page 45.

If you decide to investigate Dr. Vincent Cary, turn to page 99.

from page 34

As soon as you turn the corner, you realize what a mistake you've made. Borzoi and his accomplice over-power you.

"Another anxious customer," the accomplice says. They tie and gag you before you have a chance to shout for help.

Unable to make a sound, you can only observe helplessly. The two criminals have put Debbi in a hidden room without windows or doors. The only way in is through a cinder-block wall that they have broken through and are now in the process of rebuilding.

Now they throw you in the room next to Debbi. Neither of you can do anything as the men cement the final cinder blocks in place.

It takes you over an hour, but you finally manage to work free from the ropes. Then you quickly untie Debbi and force out a few of the freshly cemented blocks.

But it is too late to catch the criminals. You may never know what happened to the missing rock star.

THE END

from page 30

You return to the nurses' lounge where you had questioned Sissy White. No one there now seems to know where she is. She was last seen shortly after you had been there to ask questions.

Opening the hospital directory, you quickly flip through the pages and find Bill Bentwick's name. His office is on the main floor, just down the corridor from the emergency-room area.

If your suspicions are correct, you may well find Sissy White visiting Mr. Bentwick in his office.

As you enter the corridor leading to Bentwick's office, you decide to be careful. Sissy White knows you've been asking questions about Debbi Lambswood. If she sees that you are following her—if indeed you do find her at Bentwick's office—she and Bentwick might try to silence you.

You walk quickly past Bentwick's office, taking only a fast glance inside. Sissy White is standing just inside. Fortunately for you, her back is to the door and she does not see you. You only caught a quick glimpse at Bentwick.

Now you must find a place to wait, out of sight. You think that Bentwick and Sissy White, if they are involved in the disappearances of Debbi Lambswood and Bjorn Storm, will lead you to either or both of the victims.

You park yourself behind a rack of medical trays, about thirty feet down the corridor from Bentwick's office. Several minutes pass, and nothing happens. You're starting to get nervous. What if you are barking up the wrong tree?

Just as your uncertainty reaches its peak, Bentwick and Sissy White come out of the office. She walks in your direction. Bentwick turns and walks the opposite way.

If you follow Bill Bentwick, turn to page 51.

If you follow Sissy White, turn to page 64.

You decide it is time for the professionals to take over.

Returning to the emergency-room area, you approach Lieutenant Trapp, who is busy questioning a nurse.

"Just a minute," he says, when you ask to speak with him.

"It's really important," you say.

But Trapp doesn't listen. Only after he thanks the nurse for answering his questions does he finally turn to you. As quickly as you can, you tell him your whole story.

At first, Trapp seems reluctant to believe you. But because he's responsible for checking out all possible leads, he agrees to go with you to the fourth floor.

He takes his time, however, and several minutes pass before you get started.

When you get to the fourth floor, you direct Trapp to the last room on the right. He tries the doorknob and finds the door unlocked. Pushing the door open, he walks into the room.

The room is empty!

Trapp looks around and finds nothing. The room seems to be in perfect order. He storms out of the room, too annoyed even to speak to you.

You're pretty angry yourself. If Trapp had listened to you and acted quickly, you would have had the kidnappers.

Now you have to start all over.

THE END

from page 38

After making sure Debbi gets home safely, you go to Billy's Diner to have a soda and think things over.

"What possible reason," you ask yourself, "could an x-ray technician, an underworld figure, and a doctor have to kidnap a rock star?"

If only you could find a motive, you know you could solve the case. Then you could turn over all your evidence to Lieutenant Trapp.

One good way to find a motive would be to find a past relationship between Bjorn Storm and someone on your list of suspects. It may be a long shot, but you decide to go to the Oak Hills Library and spend the afternoon plowing through back issues of newspapers and magazines.

After a ten-minute walk, you arrive at the library. You decide to page through two years worth of newspaper and magazine entertainment articles. You begin this task full of energy, but after two hours your concentration begins to slip. Precious time is rushing by.

Stacks and stacks of material still await your inspection. Then, as you turn the page of a popular magazine, you are greeted by a surprise—a photo article on Bjorn Storm. In one of the photographs, Storm is leaving a restaurant with a beautiful young woman. The caption below the photograph identifies the woman as Storm's "frequent companion." No name is given, but you know exactly who she is.

The young woman in the photograph is Sissy White, the nurse who was assigned to Storm's room at Oak Hills Hospital!

Storm, you speculate, had stopped seeing Sissy. Her motive is revenge. But what do Bentwick, Borzoi, and a doctor have to do with Sissy White's broken heart?

You take from your pocket the note that Dr. Vincent Cary left for Sissy White. You compare this to the slip of paper on which Sissy wrote her friend's telephone number. The two styles of writing are similar enough to have been written by the same hand. Sissy White may have forged the note from Dr. Cary, and Debbi Lambswood might be right: Dr. Cary is not the type of person to be involved in something like this.

Borzoi, you remember, has been moving his crime organization into rock-concert promotions. You guess that he might have tried to sign up Bjorn Storm as one of his stars. If Storm refused, then Borzoi might have decided to get the rock star out of the way. If Storm couldn't keep his concert commitments, then Borzoi could step in and offer to promoters the rock stars under contract to him.

Bill Bentwick, the x-ray technician, is probably nothing more than a hired man. Sissy White, you guess, is not even aware that Bentwick is involved in the scheme. When you talked to her, she attempted to throw suspicion onto Bentwick. Without realizing that he was as involved as she, Sissy probably just went along with Debbi Lambswood's feeling that Bentwick's behavior was odd. Sissy, you reason, is being used as a pawn. The pieces of this puzzling caper are slowly coming together.

Now there's only the role of the mystery doctor to understand. Could there be a business connection between the "Doc" and Boston Borzoi? Maybe the doctor is a major investor in Borzoi's new rock-and-roll business venture.

The thing to do now is actually to find Bjorn Storm, and you think you may be able to do just that.

If you decide to finish the investigation on your own, turn to page 58.

If you decide to enlist the help of Dr. Desmond, turn to page 71.

from page 34

You tiptoe away from the sounds and squeeze into a narrow space between two large cartons. Borzoi and his accomplice take their time with what they are doing, but after several minutes, you hear their footsteps. The footsteps approach, pass you, then fade away.

Once you are sure Borzoi and his friend have left the basement, you race down the passageway. What you find is a freshly rebuilt cinder-block wall.

Borzoi and his accomplice have taken your friend Debbi Lambswood and sealed her behind a wall. You work frantically to loosen one of the blocks. Luckily the mortar is still wet. When you finally edge the block out and remove it, you can barely make out in the darkness the identity of your friend. Debbi is bound and gagged in what appears to be a windowless, hidden room. The room, you suspect, was probably the result of a mistake by the architect or builder of the hospital.

You pull out more blocks and climb into the room. Quickly, you untie your upset friend. You do your best to calm her, then carefully lead her out of the basement.

Back on the main floor of the hospital, you find Lieutenant Trapp still in the emergency-room waiting area. You go over to him with Debbi and explain all that has happened.

Trapp immediately goes into action. Within a quarter of an hour he has located and arrested both Boston Borzoi and his accomplice, who turns out to be Bill Bentwick, an x-ray technician.

It takes Trapp only a few more minutes to get the rest of the truth out of the two kidnappers. Borzoi admits that Dr. Raymond Desmond is involved and that Bjorn Storm is alive, but under heavy sedation, in a locked room on the top floor of the hospital.

Before Trapp carts all the accused off to police headquarters, he shakes your hand.

"Excellent work," he says. "You saved two lives. I appreciate that."

"Thanks, Lieutenant," you say with a smile, as you turn and escort Debbi Lambswood from the hospital.

THE END

from page 42

You duck down behind the rack of medical trays. Sissy White doesn't see you when she walks by.

As soon as she passes, you step from behind the tray rack and head the opposite way. You hurry to catch up with Bill Bentwick.

You rush through the double doors that lead to the emergency-room area. From there you catch a glimpse of Bentwick passing through another set of doors on the other side.

Walking quickly, you pass Lieutenant Trapp, who is still in the emergency-room area. You smile at him. He frowns at you.

"Don't go away, Lieutenant," you say to Trapp over your shoulder. "I'll need to speak to you in a few minutes, I think."

Before Trapp can say anything, you have passed through the doors in pursuit of Bentwick. You see that he is waiting for an elevator. Slowing down, you walk calmly to where Bentwick is standing and wait for the elevator with him and a few other people. Bentwick has never seen you, but Sissy White could have described you to him. You'll just have to take your chances.

Bentwick doesn't seem to notice you until you both get into the elevator. He studies your face. But you just smile at him, and he looks away.

You ride with Bentwick to the fourth and top floor of the hospital. He steps off the elevator quickly and turns left down the corridor. You hang back, waiting to see where he goes.

Bentwick walks all the way down to the end of the corridor and knocks lightly at the last door on the right. Someone opens the door and lets him in.

If only you had a good excuse for knocking on the door. Then you see it. Parked against one wall of the corridor is a snack cart. You decide to borrow the cart for a few minutes.

After pushing the cart down to the last room on the right, you knock loudly on the door.

"Snacks," you say loudly.

"No, thanks," calls someone from inside.

You pause for a second. Should you play it hot or cool? You decide to play it hot.

"Do you think Mr. Storm would like anything?" you ask.

The only response is silence, and that's your cue to run.

By the time the door opens, you are already back at the elevators. Bill Bentwick comes out of the room and sees you. He starts after you, almost at a run.

Without enough time to wait for an elevator, you bolt down the stairs, taking them two at a time. Your goal is the emergency-room area, where you hope to find Lieutenant Trapp.

When you get there, almost out of breath, Trapp is right where you left him. You rush over to him.

"I found where they're hiding Bjorn Storm," you blurt out.

"What?" Trapp barks.

"Come on. There's no time to lose."

Scowling, Trapp follows you to the elevators.

"This better not be some kind of a joke," he says as the two of you get into the next available car.

"It's no joke," you say, still breathing heavily.

As the elevator hits the fourth floor, you bolt out ahead of Trapp.

"Lieutenant," you say, pointing down the corridor, "Bjorn Storm, and possibly my friend Debbi Lambswood, are being held captive in the last room on the right."

"We'll see about this," Trapp says.

The lieutenant strides down to the room you have indicated and pounds on the door.

"Police," Trapp says. "Open up."

As the door opens, Trapp draws his gun. After a few seconds, you look into the room.

Bill Bentwick and another man, whom you recognize as the underworld figure Boston Borzoi, have just moved a patient, covered from head to toe in bandages, from the bed to a stretcher. Tied up in a chair is a terrified Debbi Lambswood.

While you run over to untie Debbi, Trapp finds a pair of scissors and carefully cuts the bandages away from the mummylike patient's face.

Just as you thought, the patient is Bjorn Storm.

Bjorn Storm later tells you that he had refused to perform under contract for one of Boston Borzoi's entertainment companies. Borzoi, it seems, then cooked up a plan to get Storm out of the way, enlisting members of the hospital's staff. With Storm unable to keep his concert commitments, Borzoi would attempt to fill the vacancies with "stars" under contract to his phony companies.

After all of the facts in the case have been revealed, you receive a nice phone call the next day from Lieutenant Trapp. He thanks you for your excellent detective work, and tells you that in the future he will be more open to your help on important cases.

You've scored a double victory.

THE END

Deciding to conclude this investigation on your own, you wheel your young patient down to the last door on the right.

You grab hold of the knob. To your surprise, the door is unlocked. Putting your head down, you start to push the wheelchair into the room. But what you see makes you come to a dead stop.

"What do you want?" asks Bentwick.

"I'm supposed to bring this patient to this room," you say.

"Well, go back and check again. This is a private room, and it's occupied."

"Okay," you say, backing out of the room. The door slams shut, and you hear the lock click.

It doesn't make any difference. Even though your head was down when you pushed your way into the room, your eyes were open. There was no mistaking Bjorn Storm. You caught only a quick glimpse, but he's the only person you know of who has blond hair with a dyed blue streak in it.

You rush to the fourth-floor nurses' station and ask to use the phone. You call down to the emergency room and, after waiting a couple of minutes, get Lieutenant Trapp on the line.

"Trapp speaking," the lieutenant says gruffly.

"Lieutenant, if you want to find Bjorn Storm and two of his kidnappers, come up to the fourth floor."

"Who is this?" Trapp demands.

You identify yourself and brief Trapp on your findings.

Within minutes, Lieutenant Trapp is on the fourth floor. He goes straight to the last room on the right, and demands to be let in. Then he arrests Borzoi and Bentwick. Trapp gets them to reveal the whereabouts of Debbi Lambswood.

Later, you learn that Bjorn Storm has also been arrested. It seems that he was involved in the scheme from the beginning. It was all a plan to grab publicity for the up-and-coming rock star, who had just signed a contract with one of the entertainment companies run by Boston Borzoi. Storm learned quickly, however, that crime does not pay.

THE END

You return to the hospital through a set of double doors that leads to the hospital's administrative offices. Eventually, you pass a small office with a sign that reads "Central Switchboard." The door is open, and you can hear two phone operators connecting callers to extensions throughout the hospital.

"Dr. Brown," you hear one of the operators say, "there is a Mr. Braxton on the line. Can you speak with him?" After a moment's pause she says, "Thank you. I'll connect you."

Now you have a sense of how the phone system works. You go to a public-telephone booth about thirty feet down the corridor from the switchboard office. You take out the slip of paper with the number where Sissy White can be reached.

The first time you dial, the line is busy. You wait a few minutes and try again.

"Hello," Sissy White says.

"Are you all right?" you ask.

"It's you," she says. "Yes, I'm fine. What's going on? Are you at the hospital?"

"Yes," you say, "I'm at the hospital and I've found Bjorn Storm!"

"What?" she exclaims.

"I've found him. I'm going to question him for a few minutes, then call in Lieutenant Trapp."

"Well," she says, "good work. I had no idea you were such a good detective. Congratulations."

"Thank you," you say. "I just wanted to let you know. I've got to go."

"Okay. Thanks for calling."

"'Bye," you say and hang up the phone.

Quickly, you walk to the spot just outside the switchboard office. You listen carefully.

"Good afternoon. Oak Hill Hospital," you hear an operator say. Then there is a pause.

"Dr. Desmond," the operator says, "Miss White is calling." She pauses. "Thank you, Doctor. I'll connect you."

You must hurry. You look at a directory on the wall. Desmond's office is all the way down the corridor and to the right. You head down the corridor and position yourself several feet away from the office of the chief of staff, your head over a water fountain as if to take a drink.

Within seconds, Dr. Raymond Desmond comes bursting out of his office. Rushing down the corridor, he reaches the elevators and pushes the button several times.

Now comes the hard part. You can't get on the elevator with Dr. Desmond. Sissy White may have described you to him, and he might recognize you. You'll have to run up the stairs next to the elevators and meet Desmond's elevator at each floor to see if he gets off. There are three floors above you.

You rush up the stairs to the second floor and peek through the door to the stairway. The elevator stops and a nurse gets on. Dr. Desmond does not get off. Neither does he get off at the third floor.

Now you know that Dr. Desmond is going to the fourth floor. You wait in the stairway. Holding the door open a crack, you hear the elevator door open and then close.

You step out into the hallway in time to see Desmond turn down the corridor to the left. You go up to the corner Desmond just turned. The hospital chief of staff walks quickly to the end of the corridor and enters the last room on the right.

Your plan has worked. You are certain that Bjorn Storm is in the room Dr. Desmond just entered.

Your first instinct is to race into the room after Desmond, but that kind of move might expose you to danger.

Instead, you use a hall phone to call down to Lieutenant Trapp in the emergency-room area. You tell him that you have found Bjorn Storm on the fourth floor. You give Trapp the location of the room.

"I'm on my way!" Trapp says.

But what if you have guessed wrong all the way down the line? What if Bjorn Storm is *not* in the room? If you are wrong, your reputation as an amateur detective will be mud. You must find out if Storm is in the room *before* Trapp arrives.

Slowly, you walk toward the room. When you get there, you find the door closed. You push the door open a crack.

The method of Dr. Desmond's madness is plainly visible. The doctor is standing next to the bed of a patient who is completely covered with bandages. Only the patient's eyes, nose, and mouth are visible. Bjorn Storm has been wrapped up like a mummy. He is, no doubt, under Dr. Desmond's personal care!

Suddenly, you are shoved into the room from behind. Turning around, you see that Boston Borzoi has joined the party. The only difference is that he has a gun, and it's pointed at you.

"Is this the kid, Doc?" Borzoi asks.

"Yes," Dr. Desmond says. "Fits the description I have."

"Well, how about if we wrap up the kid just like our friend the rock star?" Borzoi says.

Just as Borzoi utters his last word, the door flies open.

"Drop it, Borzoi," says Lieutenant Trapp.

Borzoi lets his gun fall to the floor.

"Okay, Dr. Desmond," Trapp says. "Why don't we unwrap the rock star, pronto."

In no time, the bandages are removed. Bjorn Storm is all right, even though he is still asleep from the sedative Dr. Desmond must have given him.

You take Lieutenant Trapp aside and tell him about Bill Bentwick and Sissy White. The lieutenant thanks you and shakes your hand.

"Nice job," he says.

THE END

from page 42

You wait until Sissy White is well past your hiding place. Then you follow her. She turns right into another corridor.

You hesitate for a few seconds before making the turn yourself. As soon as you do make the turn, you regret it.

Sissy White is standing right around the corner, flanked on either side by hospital security guards.

"That's the one," she says, pointing right at you. "Been snooping around the hospital all day and doesn't belong here."

The two guards come over to you and grab you by the arms.

"Come on," one of them says. "You don't belong here."

"But . . . ." you say.

"Now don't make a fuss, or you'll be in real trouble," the other guard says.

You are escorted out of the hospital and told not to return. Your investigation has been abruptly terminated. Lieutenant Trapp will have to solve this case without you.

THE END

66

Bentwick's office, you learn from the hospital's directory, is on the ground floor. You'll use the easiest trick you can think of to strike up a conversation with him.

You push the wheelchair down to Bentwick's office and knock on the door. From within, someone (you assume it is Bentwick) tells you to come in.

"You sent for a wheelchair?" you say as you poke your head into the office.

"No, I didn't," says the young man behind the desk.

"No?" you say, playing dumb.

"Nope," he says, smiling, but with a hint of annoyance in his voice. You won't be sent away that easily, however.

"Have you heard the latest about that rock star?" you say, removing your false glasses to clean them.

"What about him?" Bentwick says.

"Well, I heard that he snuck out of the hospital without paying his bill, and that he took along that pretty nurse's aide who's missing," you say, making up a story so improbable that Bentwick will have to believe that *you* believe it.

As you were speaking, you watched Bentwick's face. He reacted normally, until you made your reference to Debbi Lambswood. As far as you know, no one but you and her kidnappers know that she is missing. But when you mentioned her, even without using her name, Bentwick's cool expression changed. You anticipate Bentwick's next words.

"Where did you hear that story about the nurse's aide?" he asks.

"Around," you say as you turn to leave.

"Around where?" Bentwick demands, jumping up from behind his desk. He follows you into the hallway.

"Around the hospital," you say as you push the wheelchair away.

Bentwick rushes back into his office and slams the door shut. You have a feeling that Mr. Bentwick may be on the phone with a fellow kidnapper.

If you attempt to listen to Bentwick's phone conversation, turn to page 26.

If you decide to wait for Bentwick to leave his office and then follow him, turn to page 76.

from page 23

You walk right into Dr. Desmond's outer office. His secretary is not at her desk, so you knock on the closed door of his inner office.

The door swings open.

"Can I help you?" Dr. Desmond says.

"Yes, I hope so," you say. "I have information that could lead to the rescue of Bjorn Storm, the missing rock star."

"Well, come right in," Desmond says. "I'd be very interested to hear what you have to say."

You take a seat and say hello to Boston Borzoi, without giving a hint that you know who he is.

"Now," Dr. Desmond says, "what sort of information do you have?"

You tell him about the call you received early this morning from Debbi Lambswood, and how she was suddenly cut off before she could finish talking. But, you say, she did tell you that she suspected that members of the hospital staff were involved.

"Is that so?" Dr. Desmond says. "This interests me very much. I'm very glad you came to talk to me." With that, Dr. Desmond excuses himself from the office, saying that he will be right back.

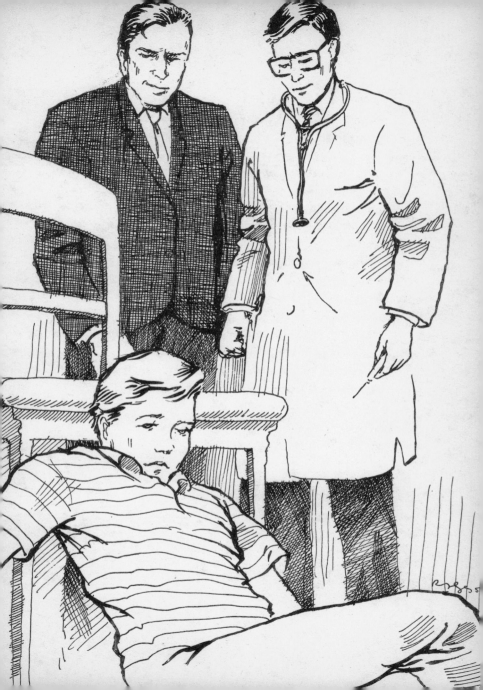

Now Borzoi looks you in the eye, and a slight chill passes through you.

"This sounds pretty serious," Borzoi says.

You begin to answer him when you feel a sudden stinging sensation in your arm. Turning your head quickly, you see the smiling face of Dr. Desmond as he withdraws an empty hypodermic needle from your shoulder.

"Just a little something to calm your nerves," Desmond says. "You'll feel much better in a few seconds."

He's right. You feel so relaxed that you slide off the chair onto the floor. The room begins to spin. You will sleep right through the investigation.

Now it's up to Lieutenant Trapp. You hope he isn't too far behind you in *his* investigation.

THE END

from page 48

When you arrive back at the hospital, you go immediately to Dr. Raymond Desmond's office. You tell his secretary that you must discuss a life-and-death matter with the chief of staff. She buzzes him on the intercom, and he instructs her to send you right in.

Dr. Desmond, a tall, distinguished-looking man, greets you and invites you to sit down.

"How can I help you?" he asks. You tell the hospital's chief doctor all that you have found out, naming the three people—Bentwick, Borzoi, and Sissy White—you already believe are involved. Then you shock him with the news that a doctor from the hospital may also be involved.

"Who?" he asks.

"I haven't figured that out yet," you say. "That's why I've come to you. Sissy White tried to throw suspicion on Dr. Vincent Cary, but I'm almost certain that it's not he."

"Certainly not," Desmond says. "Vince Cary is as honest as any man I know."

Dr. Desmond purses his lips and rubs his temples with his fingertips.

"Why don't you join me while I check in on a patient," Desmond says. "We can talk about this on the way. After I finish with the patient, we can get in touch with Lieutenant Trapp. By the way, can I get you a soda before we go?"

"Sure," you say.

Dr. Desmond steps out of the office and returns a minute later with a paper cup filled with fizzing cola.

"Thank you," you say.

"You're quite welcome," he says.

Dr. Desmond waits until you finish your soda. Then the two of you leave his office together. You both ride the elevator to the fourth floor of the hospital. You turn left and walk down the corridor. The room of Dr. Desmond's patient is the last one on the right.

Inside, you see that the unconscious patient is bandaged from head to foot, looking something like a mummy.

"Poor fellow had a terrible accident," Desmond says, leaning over the patient.

"What happened to him?" you ask.

"He got in the way," he says, "just as you did."

Suddenly you are confused. The room has begun to change shape, and you feel dizzy.

You fall to your knees, but Dr. Desmond helps you onto the other bed. Before you lose consciousness, you realize that the bandaged person is Bjorn Storm, and that the doctor involved in the crime is none other than Raymond Desmond.

Just before you pass out, you look Desmond in the eye and say groggily, "You put something in the soda."

"That's correct," he says as all goes dark.

THE END

74

You call the best hotel in town, assuming that Storm's band must be registered there. The desk clerk confirms your assumption, and you head over to the hotel.

When you get there, you call up to the room of Andy Bangs, the bass player, and ask if you can come up to talk.

"About what?" the musician asks with irritation.

"About what happened to Mr. Storm last night," you say.

"Okay," he says and hangs up the phone.

When Bangs lets you into his room, you see why he was so short with you. Some rock stars like to sleep late —and you have awakened him.

"Do you know of anyone who had something to gain from Bjorn Storm's injury?" you ask.

"Sure," he says, laughing. "The entire rock-music world. Bjorn's getting so popular, he's drawing all the attention his way. Everybody is jealous of his success."

"Including members of his own band?" you ask.

"Maybe," Bangs says coolly.

"How about you?"

"Could be, but I'm not the type to hurt someone. Besides, Bjorn has always taken care of me."

"Is there anyone in the band who doesn't feel that way?"

"No comment," Bangs answers.

"It would make things a lot easier if you answered my question. I think that Bjorn Storm's life is in danger."

"Okay, okay. Talk to Kevin, our drummer. He's in the next room. He and Bjorn really hate each other."

"Thanks a lot," you say, as you leave Andy Bangs' room.

Turn to page 82.

76

from page 67

You wait at the far end of the corridor for Bentwick to leave his office. When he finally emerges, you step back around the corner. Bentwick heads toward a stairwell.

Leaving your wheelchair behind, you rush over to the stairwell. Bentwick is out of sight, but you can hear his footsteps. He's headed for the basement.

You follow on tiptoes. The last thing you want now is to give yourself away.

Carefully, you slip through the fire door and into the basement passageway. There is no one else down here, and you can still hear Bentwick's footsteps trailing off to the right.

You follow, still making every effort not be heard. The basement is laid out so that large, locked doors, each marked "Storage Rooms," can be reached by narrow passageways.

Suddenly, Bentwick's footsteps stop.

"Well, it's nice to see you're still safe and sound," you hear Bentwick say. But no one responds.

Now you hear Bentwick start to walk back up the passageway toward you.

If you hide in the passageway and hope Bentwick doesn't see you, turn to page 85.

If you rush back up the stairs, hoping to follow Bentwick from there, turn to page 90.

from page 81

As soon as Borzoi is out of sight, you walk right into Dr. Desmond's outer office. You find him standing next to an open filing cabinet. His back is to you.

"Dr. Desmond," you say.

He turns with a start. "Yes?" he says.

"Can we talk?" you ask.

"Regarding what?"

"Bjorn Storm, the missing rock star."

"Well," Dr. Desmond says, "may I ask how that matter concerns you?"

You tell the chief of staff all about the suddenly interrupted call you had from Debbi Lambswood. You mention her suspicion of unknown members of the hospital staff.

"Very interesting," says Dr. Desmond. "I want to know what else you've learned. Can you wait right here for a minute? I'll be right back."

"Sure," you say.

You do not know what to think. Dr. Desmond seems honest enough. Perhaps Borzoi is here for a reason unrelated to Bjorn Storm's disappearance. Maybe Borzoi makes charitable contributions to the hospital, to give himself an image of respectability.

A few minutes later, when Desmond returns to the office, he is followed by Boston Borzoi and a member of the hospital's staff. Borzoi closes the door behind him, then takes out a gun from his pocket.

For you, this may be . . .

THE END

from page 15

So many questions are in your mind that you wonder whether or not you should leave this case to professionals. If you weren't concerned about Debbi, you would probably go home right now.

Instead, you go to the hospital's main desk. You ask the woman at the desk where you can find Pappy at this hour. She tells you that he lives in a rooming house just a few blocks from the hospital.

Once again, as you are about to leave the hospital, you catch a glimpse of Boston Borzoi. This time, however, you see that he is talking to a doctor. Keeping your distance from the conversation, you stop a hospital orderly and quietly ask him to identify the doctor.

"That's Dr. Vincent Cary, our top surgeon," he says.

You thank the orderly and write down the information in your notebook. Then you go to find Pappy's house.

When you knock on the door to Pappy's room, you are greeted by the old custodian's roaring voice.

"Who is it?" he asks.

You identify yourself and your business.

"So they haven't found that young pop star, eh?" Pappy says as he opens the door. "They may never find him. He's probably right there in the hospital, but they may never find him."

"What do you mean?" you ask.

"My grandfather helped build that hospital. He told me that the builders made some mistakes. There are all sorts of hidden rooms down in the basement. In other words, there are places down there that almost no one knows about. Now if I was going to hide somebody, I'd use one of those rooms."

"Do you know how to get into those rooms?" you ask.

"No, I do not," Pappy says.

"Do you know of anyone who does?"

"Yes, I do. Two people, in fact."

"Who?" you ask.

"Dr. Raymond Desmond, head of the hospital, and Bill Bentwick, that fresh, young x-ray technician. The doctor knows, because he told me he did. Now, how young Bentwick found out, I don't know, but I saw him down in the basement one day. He was snooping around, and I overheard him ask another janitor where the hidden rooms were. I'm sure he's found them by now."

You write this down and ask, "What about this Bentwick? You had an argument with him last night?"

"Oh, he's loony. He just came on the staff, and he's already into everybody's business."

"How do you mean?"

"He's nosy—always asking questions about things that don't concern him."

"Do you think he could be involved in the disappearance of Bjorn Storm?"

"I suppose he could be," Pappy says.

As you leave, you thank Pappy and tell him that you might want to talk to him later.

If you decide to check the hospital's basement for hidden rooms, turn to page 29.

If you decide that it's time to question Bill Bentwick, turn to page 25.

from page 23

You decide to wait. It's too early in your investigation to approach powerful men like Dr. Desmond and Borzoi while they are together. You're not even sure of your facts yet.

Fortunately, you know how to make yourself look as if you belong where you don't. You pull out your notebook and pretend to take notes from the papers posted on the bulletin board.

You manage to keep cool for about twenty minutes. Suddenly Borzoi leaves Desmond's office, then heads out through the double doors. Desmond stands in the doorway to his office, watches Borzoi leave, then goes back inside.

If you follow Borzoi, turn to page 33.

If you go into Desmond's office to question him, turn to page 77.

from page 75

You knock on the drummer's door.

You hear sounds of movement inside the room. Then the door opens.

"What's up?" Kevin asks.

"Can I talk to you about Bjorn Storm's accident?"

"Come on in," he says.

You enter the room, and Kevin opens the drapes to let in some light. The drummer, like Andy Bangs, is still in his bathrobe.

"So what can I tell you?" Kevin asks.

"Do you know of anyone who might like to see Bjorn Storm out of the way?"

"Me, for one," Kevin says.

"Why?" you ask.

"Because Bjorn hogs the limelight. He acts like the rest of us in the band don't count, and he makes decisions that aren't in the band's best interest."

"What kind of decisions?"

"Well, he's made some bad choices in financial matters—like refusing to join up with some very powerful interests."

"Can you explain?" you ask.

"I'd better let a friend of mine do that," Kevin says, reaching for the phone.

"Just hang on a second," he says to you as he dials a number.

"Is B. B. there?" Kevin asks into the phone. There is a pause, then he speaks again.

"Hey, B. B., this is Kevin. Say, there's a kid here who seems very interested in Bjorn's whereabouts, and seems to know a lot about what happened." Kevin pauses, then says, "Okay, we'll wait." Then the drummer hangs up the phone.

"Wait around. Somebody is coming by who will answer all your questions."

This doesn't feel quite right to you, and you consider leaving. But you have to get to the bottom of this case.

You and Kevin talk about the rock-music world for close to ten minutes. Then you are interrupted by a loud knock at the door.

Kevin opens the door, and in walks a sinister-looking character whose face you recognize from the newspapers. The man is Boston Borzoi, a notorious underworld figure.

"Is this the one?" Borzoi asks.

"Sure is," Kevin says.

"Well," Borzoi says, turning to you, "why don't you come with me? My car is right outside."

You don't want to go, but something about Borzoi's eyes tells you you have no choice.

You follow Borzoi outside to a long black limousine with a mean-looking chauffeur at the wheel. Borzoi opens the back door for you and you get in. Then Borzoi slams the door without getting in himself. You hear a click as both doors lock.

With a silly grin, Borzoi looks through the window at you and waves goodbye. You are cut off from the front seat and the chauffeur by a thick glass divider.

Then the limo pulls away. You don't know what is going to happen to you, but you don't want to wait to find out. Whatever you decide to do, you're sure you'll have only once chance to do it.

If you decide to try to outsmart the chauffeur, turn to page 113.

If you decide to try to get help from the drivers of other cars on the road, turn to page 115.

from page 76

Just in time to escape Bentwick's notice, you slide in between some large cartons and hope for the best.

Bentwick passes by. As soon as he's gone, you turn down the passageway he just came from.

To your surprise, the passage leads to a dead end. You remember that when Bentwick stood here, he said: "It's nice to see you're still safe and sound."

What did he mean? You run your hands along the cinder-block wall in a desperate attempt to find a clue. For once, desperation pays off.

The mortar between the blocks is fresh! The wall was recently built or rebuilt, and you believe that there is something—or somebody—behind it.

With nimble fingers, you scrape out the wet mortar from around one of the blocks. Grabbing the edge of the loose block with your fingertips, you use all of your strength to pull it slowly out of the wall.

It is pitch dark inside. But by the light in the hall, you can barely make out that a person is inside. The person is your friend Debbi Lambswood! Her mouth is covered with tape; her hands and feet are bound with rope.

After quickly pulling out more blocks, you enter the windowless room and untie Debbi.

"Are you okay?" you ask.

"I'm all right," she says. "I'm scared, but I just knew you would find me."

"Let's go to the police right now," you say.

You take Debbi up to the emergency room and let her tell her story to Trapp.

Within minutes, Trapp finds Bentwick and arrests him. And in an effort to save himself, Bentwick leads Trapp to Boston Borzoi, who is holding the missing rock star, Bjorn Storm.

Your good work has saved the day.

THE END

Borzoi and Bentwick walk back through the emergency-room area. They head toward the administrative offices. You follow them through double doors labeled "Authorized Personnel Only."

Without hesitation, the two men walk into an office. You pass by the office and keep watching. The nameplate next to the door reads "Raymond Desmond, M.D., Chief of Staff."

If you decide to listen outside the office door, turn to page 89.

If you walk right into the office, ready to say something that will shock all those who are guilty, turn to page 98.

from page 24

You decide to find the hospital worker who pretended to be an electrician. He may be the key to your whole investigation.

"Tall, thin, young, and he has brown hair," you say, describing the man to a nurse whom you stop in a corridor.

"Oh, yes," she replies, "that sounds very much like Bill Bentwick, a member of our x-ray department."

You thank the nurse for her help, then look up Bentwick's name in the hospital directory. Bentwick's office is located on the main floor. Now that you know where he is, you have to decide how to deal with him.

If you decide to keep him under surveillance, turn to page 100.

If you decide to approach him directly, turn to page 105.

You carefully walk over and stand three or four feet to the right of the doorway. You lean back against the wall and listen.

The three men are talking, but barely above a whisper. You move closer to the door.

Suddenly, Bentwick pokes his head out of the doorway and spots you.

"Come on in," he says, as he grabs you by the shoulder and yanks you into the office. Then all goes dark. For you this may spell . . .

THE END

from page 76

You rush up the stairs, trying to remain undetected. When you reach the ground floor, you yank open the door to the stairwell.

In your path stands a man whose face you have seen before. It's Boston Borzoi, the underworld figure.

"Who are you?" he asks, pushing you back into the stairwell and letting the door close behind him.

"I just work here," you say.

Unfortunately for you, Bentwick arrives from the basement.

"That's the kid who knew about the missing nurse's aide," he says to Borzoi as soon as he sees you.

"Oh, yeah?" Borzoi says. "Well, I got a funny feeling about this kid."

Bentwick slaps his hand across your mouth and Borzoi twists your arm behind you.

Then they take you back down to the basement. They tie you up and gag you, and lock you in a dark storage room. You hope Lieutenant Trapp finds you soon.

THE END

92

from page 98

"Lieutenant Trapp," you say to the tall police detective.

"Yes?"

"In about five minutes I will be able to lead you to Bjorn Storm."

Trapp squints at you suspiciously. "What are you talking about?" he asks.

"Can you wait five minutes to find out?"

"Sure," he says, with amusement.

You leave Trapp and walk over to the double doors that lead to the administrative area. Opening the doors a crack, you see Borzoi, Bentwick, and Desmond standing nervously near the elevators.

You wave for Trapp to join you. Just as he does, the three suspects get into the elevator.

"We've got to hurry now," you say to Trapp as you bolt through the doors toward the elevators.

Trapp is on your heels.

You get to the elevators and watch the floor indicator. The car stops on only one floor, the fourth. You and Trapp get into the next available car and take it to that floor.

You step out into the fourth-floor hallway and peek around the corner. At the end of the corridor, Dr. Desmond unlocks the door to the last room on the right. Borzoi and Bentwick follow Dr. Desmond into the room.

"Bjorn Storm should be in the last room on the right," you say to Lieutenant Trapp.

"You'd better be right," Trapp says as he strides down the corridor. Trapp knocks on the door.

"Police," he calls as he turns the doorknob. "Open the door."

The door is unlocked. Trapp pushes it open and steps inside.

The three suspects are speechless. In a hospital bed is a sleeping patient covered from head to toe in bandages.

"Is that Bjorn Storm inside those bandages?" asks Trapp.

No one answers.

"You three are under arrest," Trapp says. He turns his head toward you and nods appreciatively.

You have solved a tough case.

THE END

from page 98

It may be too soon to bring in Lieutenant Trapp. Suppose he pays no attention to you, and tells you to go away? Even worse, suppose you are wrong?

You wait on the other side of the double doors, holding them open just a crack. Through the crack, you see the three suspects—Borzoi, Bentwick, and Dr. Desmond —leave Desmond's office and head toward the elevators.

When they board the first available car, you rush over and watch the floor indicator. The suspects' elevator goes directly to the fourth, and top, floor of the hospital.

You take the next available car and go right to the fourth floor. You arrive in time to see the three men enter the last room on the right down the corridor.

As the door to the room closes, you walk quickly toward it. You put your ear to the door and listen.

Suddenly, the door swings open. Boston Borzoi grabs you by the collar and yanks you into the room. He slams the door shut.

"That was a pretty funny trick you played on us," he says.

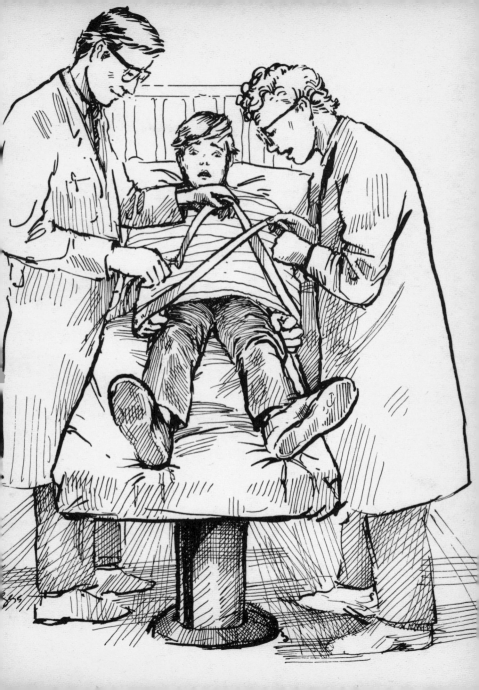

"Gee," you say, trying to think fast. "I'm glad you liked it."

"A real smart aleck," Borzoi says as he grabs you.

Bill Bentwick steps toward you with an armful of bandages. Before you know it, the men wrap you up like a mummy. They put you onto a hospital bed. You look over and see that a patient on the other bed in the room is already totally bandaged like a mummy.

"So that's what they did with Bjorn Storm," you mutter to yourself. Now you have to find your way out of the same exact mess as the missing rock star.

THE END

from page 25

"Excuse me," you say loudly. Borzoi and Bentwick turn around together.

"Yeah, what is it?" Borzoi asks.

"Does either of you know Debbie Lambswood?" you ask.

"Of course," Bentwick replies. "She's our friend. Are you looking for her?"

"Yes, but she seems to have disappeared."

"Are you sure about that? We just saw her, and she's fine," says Bentwick.

"We could take you right to her," Borzoi says.

You don't like this at all. You turn and walk away. Then you start to walk faster and faster, dodging through the other people in the corridor.

You leave the hospital through the first exit you find. You've blown your investigation. Borzoi and Bentwick are on the lookout for you now, and you don't have enough evidence against them to go to Lieutenant Trapp. You decide to go home and come up with a new plan.

THE END

from page 87

Calling on all of your talent as an actor, you smile and pretend to walk by Dr. Desmond's office.

But you stop in mid-stride and turn toward the office door. Three men—Borzoi, Bentwick, and, you presume, Dr. Desmond—are standing just inside.

With your biggest smile still in place, you poke your head through the doorway.

"Isn't it great," you say, "Bjorn Storm's been found!"

The three men react in a peculiar way. Their jaws drop, their eyes widen, and they are speechless.

"Guilty," you say to yourself, as you quickly leave the office. You are gone before the men have a chance to realize what happened.

You are sure that their next move will be to find out if your statement is true. First they will catch their breath. Then they will unknowingly lead you right to Bjorn Storm.

If you think it's time to call on Lieutenant Trapp, turn to page 92.

If you want to follow the suspects on your own, turn to page 94.

"Dr. Cary?" you ask the man seated behind the desk.

"Yes," the doctor says.

You introduce yourself and say that you would like to talk to him for a minute or two.

"Sure," he says. "Sit down."

You decide to trust Dr. Cary. Debbi told you he was a good person, and your own first impression tells you the same.

"Do you realize that the man you were speaking to in the emergency room today was Boston Borzoi, the underworld figure?" you ask.

Dr. Cary looks at you with an odd expression. "Well," he says, "now that you mention it, I do remember seeing that man somewhere before. Maybe I saw his picture in a newspaper."

Dr. Cary checks his watch.

"I'd like to talk to you about this, but I'm expected back in surgery in five minutes," he says, getting up to leave. "Why don't you stop back in a few hours? We can talk then."

You leave the office with Dr. Cary, and he hurries away.

If you decide to find out if Dr. Cary is telling the truth, turn to page 104.

If you decide to tell Lieutenant Trapp what you know about Bill Bentwick and Boston Borzoi, turn to page 111.

from page 88

Since Bill Bentwick does not know that you suspect him, confronting him will only put him on the defensive. You decide to hang back and keep an eye on him. Let Bentwick make the first mistake.

Like a patient hunter, you park yourself in a folding chair several yards down the corridor from Bentwick's office. Even though you don't belong in this part of the hospital, no one on the staff questions your presence. You probably appear to be quite innocent.

After about forty minutes, there is still no sign of Bentwick. You wonder if you are wasting precious time.

Suddenly, the office door opens, and the tall young man with brown hair walks out. He turns and walks away in a hurry. You wait a few seconds, then follow after Bentwick in hot pursuit.

Bentwick's path takes you through the emergency-room area, where you pass by Lieutenant Trapp. He is still questioning hospital staffers. The x-ray technician bursts through a set of double doors that lead to the administrative offices.

Bentwick enters an office to the left. You pass by, and read the name outside the door: "Raymond Desmond, M.D., Chief of Staff.

No sooner have you passed the office than Bentwick walks back out, followed by an older doctor, presumably Dr. Desmond. They pass you and go to the elevators.

Staying off to the side, you wait for them to get into the next available elevator. At the last second, you squeeze into the car with them. Bentwick and the doctor ride all the way to the fourth and top floor. Without noticing you, they get off the elevator and turn down the corridor. You watch as they enter the last door on the right.

You walk to a nearby nurses' station and ask to use the phone. Calling down to the emergency room, you manage to get Lieutenant Trapp on the phone.

"Lieutenant?" you say.

"Yes?" he replies.

"I think you may find Bjorn Storm in a room on the fourth floor."

Trapp asks you to explain. After you do, he agrees to come to the fourth floor and check things out for himself.

No sooner have you hung up the phone than Bentwick, the doctor, and another man leave the room together. You recognize the third man from his picture in the newspaper. He is Boston Borzoi, a notorious underworld leader.

When Trapp arrives in the elevator, the three men get in as he gets out.

"Did you see those three men who got in as you got out," you ask Trapp.

"Yes," Trapp says.

"Well, if my theory is right, they're all in on this together. They all just came out of the last room on the right," you say.

Trapp doesn't look convinced, but he walks over to the nurses' station and shows his police shield. He asks for and receives the passkey for all of the rooms on the floor.

Then, without saying a word to you, he strides down the corridor and opens the last door on the right.

You follow him into the room. There you see an unconscious patient bandaged from head to foot. There is no chart at the foot of the bed.

Trapp arches an eyebrow. Searching around the room, he finds a pair of scissors and cuts away some of the head bandages.

"It's Storm all right. Now who were those three men?"

You tell Trapp who the men were. He picks up the phone, calls down to the emergency room, and describes the three suspects to one of his officers. "Apprehend these men and hold them for questioning," he says.

Then Trapp turns to you: "How did you figure this out?"

You explain about the call from Debbi Lambswood and your trip to the high-school auditorium.

"Well, you did a good job," Trapp admits, "and we'll find out about your friend Debbi Lambswood in just a few minutes."

You've solved this case quickly and efficiently.

THE END

from page 99

You want to trust Dr. Vincent Cary, but he left so abruptly that it made you suspicious. You decide to follow him.

You turn a corner, and see the doctor pass through a set of doors with a sign that reads "Restricted Area. Do Not Enter."

Not wanting to lose the trail, you ignore the sign and walk through the doors. It takes you only a few seconds to realize that you are in the preparatory area near the operating rooms. Dr. Cary told you the truth.

But that bit of information won't do you any good now. A security guard saw you enter the restricted area and is walking toward you.

"What's the big idea?" he asks. "Didn't you see the sign outside this area?"

"Well, I . . ."

"Well, you nothing," the guard says. "Let's get going out of the hospital right now." He grabs you by the arm. "Next time you come here, pay attention to the rules," the guard says as he ushers you out through the back entrance.

Your investigation has been derailed. You'll call Lieutenant Trapp from home and tell him everything you've learned up to now. You hope that Trapp will use your information to solve the case. Too bad you can't be in on it till . . .

THE END

from page 88

"Hi," you say, poking your head into Bill Bentwick's office.

"What can I do for you?" the lean young man inside asks in a friendly manner.

"I was wondering," you say, "if you would please explain to me what you were doing in the high-school auditorium yesterday afternoon."

Bentwick doesn't answer immediately. He just stares at you. You notice that his face has reddened slightly.

"That's a very personal and complicated matter," he says. "I'm not sure I can explain it to you."

"Would it help if I asked Lieutenant Trapp to discuss it with you?" you say.

"Now wait a minute," Bentwick says. "I haven't done anything wrong. Come with me and I'll show you what the problem is."

You follow Bentwick from the office and go with him to the other end of the hospital. He leads you down a corridor and, using a pass key, opens a utility room.

You follow him into the room, which is filled with cleaning equipment. Sitting in a wheelchair is an unconscious patient entirely wrapped in bandages.

Amazed, you go over to the mummy in the wheel-chair. Examining the patient's unbandaged hands, you notice that the fingertips of the left hand are heavily callused. You have seen calluses like that before—on the fingertips of guitar players.

Without turning around, you say, "Is this Bjorn Storm?"

"You guessed it," Bentwick says. Now you turn, only to find yourself looking down the barrel of a revolver.

"And you're going to be his roommate for a while," Bentwick says, as he slaps a large piece of adhesive tape across your mouth.

Your only hope is that Lieutenant Trapp will find you soon.

THE END

from page 117

Trapp is still in the emergency-room area, where he has been questioning people since you arrived. You go up to him and tap on his arm.

"Yes?" Trapp says, turning toward you.

"I think I've solved this case," you say.

"What?"

Quickly and efficiently, you tell Trapp everything you've learned. You get his attention when you begin with Debbi Lambswood's interrupted phone call. Then you discuss your trip to the high-school auditorium and what you found there.

Finally, you tell Trapp about Bill Bentwick, his masquerade as an electrician at the auditorium, and the reports that he is in debt to members of the underworld.

"Sounds as though you may have solved this case," Trapp says. "Let's pay Mr. Bentwick a visit."

When you get to Bill Bentwick's office, Trapp asks you if you would mind waiting outside. You nod in agreement, and Trapp goes into Bentwick's office, closing the door behind him.

Several minutes later, the door opens and Bill Bentwick walks out in handcuffs. Trapp is behind him.

"He's confessed to everything," Trapp says. "He told me where Storm and your friend Miss Lambswood are and who the other kidnappers are. You've done a super job. Thanks."

Trapp takes Bill Bentwick away. Your career as an amateur detective has reached new heights. You may even get free front-row seats to Bjorn Storm's next concert.

THE END

from page 117

Before you bring your information to Trapp, you decide to give Bill Bentwick a chance to explain himself. You go to his office and poke your head inside the door.

"Can I help you?" Bentwick asks.

"I'd like to ask you a question or two," you say with a smile.

"Okay," Bentwick says. "About what?"

"About the missing rock star, Bjorn Storm," you say, as you close the office door behind you.

Bentwick's face shows only a trace of surprise, but he doesn't say anything for several seconds.

"Well, yes, I know a great deal about Storm. I've been working on the case myself," Bentwick says, finally.

"*You're* working on the case?" you ask. "In what capacity?"

"Just turn around," says Bentwick, "and open the second file drawer from the top. Look for the folder labeled 'Rock Performers.'"

You do as Bentwick suggests. Just as you reach into the file, however, Bentwick claps his hand across your mouth and twists your right arm behind you.

Within seconds, Bentwick has placed a gag in your mouth and tied your hands.

Your role in the case has now reached . . .

THE END

from page 99

You didn't learn anything one way or another from Dr. Cary. You still don't see a motive for the kidnapping of Bjorn Storm. But you do know that Boston Borzoi and Bill Bentwick are involved, and that they also abducted Debbi Lambswood.

Thanks to you, Debbi is now safe. Her testimony, along with your own eyewitness account, will be enough to convict Borzoi and Bentwick.

You decide to take all of your findings directly to Lieutenant Trapp.

Trapp is still in the emergency-room area. You go up to him and tell him the whole story, from Debbi's early-morning phone call to the brief conversation you just had with Dr. Cary.

"They buried that young girl alive, behind a wall?" Trapp asks.

"Yes, sir," you say.

"Why didn't you tell me sooner?" Trapp asks.

"I only wanted to . . ." you start.

"Well, thanks for your help. You'd better head on home now. We'll take it from here."

"But . . ." you begin to say in protest.

"No buts," Trapp says. "Go home now and wait for a call from me."

You turn and leave. You didn't get the chance to see your investigation through to the end. But that's okay. You're glad you were able to rescue Debbi. And you're glad to have done the crucial legwork for Lieutenant Trapp (even if he does get all the glory).

You are always on the alert for new cases and new mysteries. Next time, you have a feeling, Lieutenant Trapp will welcome your assistance.

THE END

If you are going to outwit this hard-boiled chauffeur, you're going to have to do it smoothly. He doesn't look like someone who would fall for just any trick.

As the limo heads out of town on a back road, you try to come up with a plan that might have a chance. Within minutes it comes to you.

Noticing that the chauffeur is checking on you in the rear-view mirror, you clutch your throat. You try to show that you are experiencing some discomfort. As soon as you see, from the corner of your eye, that he is watching you more carefully, you begin to roll your eyes around.

Tightening the muscles in your neck and face, you pretend that you can't breathe. Your face becomes flaming red.

The chauffeur begins to show concern. Taking out your pad and pencil, you scrawl "Can't breathe" onto a slip of paper. You hold the paper up against the glass divider.

As soon as the chauffeur reads your message, you collapse down onto the floor, out of his view.

You can almost feel his hesitation. Then you are jolted as he slams on the brakes and the limo comes to a stop.

The front door opens, and you feel the weight of the car shift as the chauffeur gets out. You don't move. The back door opens.

"Are you all right?" the chauffeur asks. He reaches down, pulls you from the floor of the limo, and places your limp body down on the shoulder of the road. The chauffeur lifts each of your eyelids. But your eyes just stare blankly at the sky.

The chauffeur rushes back into the limo and gets on his two-way radio. Not waiting to hear what he has to say, you jump to your feet and bolt into the nearby woods. The driver starts running after you, but he is clearly out of shape. He soon gives up in disgust and goes back to the limo.

It's an hour before you finally get out of the woods and find a pay phone. You get through to Lieutenant Trapp and tell him your story.

He sends out a squad car to pick you up. By the time you get back to Oak Hills, Trapp has located and arrested Kevin, the drummer in Bjorn Storm's rock group. But Boston Borzoi is nowhere to be found. And Bjorn Storm? Well, Lieutenant Trapp and his team continue to look for both him and Debbi Lambswood.

Your investigation exposed the kidnapping plot, but the kidnappers are still at large. And their victims have not been found.

THE END

from page 84

Figuring that this chauffeur has probably seen every trick in the book, you decide to try to get the attention of other drivers on the road. You hope they will see your predicament, take down the license-plate number of the limo, and call the police.

When the chauffeur stops the limo at an intersection for a red light, you begin waving your hands at other drivers. You pound on the window and mouth the words "help me!" in the direction of several motorists.

But not one of them, that you can tell, gets the message. You notice that they avert their eyes and shake their heads disapprovingly. They think that you are some spoiled rich kid throwing a tantrum!

You look at the chauffeur. He is playing his part perfectly. With an embarrassed look, he justs shrugs. He's playing for the sympathy of the other motorists.

Then the light changes, and the limo speeds away, leaving the people who would have helped you in the dust.

The chauffeur catches your eye in the rear-view mirror. You watch his reflection as he mouths the phrase "nice try."

You've used your only chance to get away. The other drivers just couldn't imagine what you might have to complain about if you were being driven around in a limousine.

Now you're off on the longest drive, it seems, of your life. Admittedly, the chauffeur chooses some very scenic country roads. But you would prefer to be back in Oak Hills cracking this case.

Several hours after dusk, the chauffeur drops you off just outside town. You know that the kidnappers have all fled, but you hope at least that Bjorn Storm and your friend Debbi Lambswood are all right.

THE END

Billy Bentwick, as the young nurse referred to him, is one of the hospital's best x-ray technicians. You learn this from a member of his department, who also comments that Bentwick occasionally gets on his co-workers' nerves. With a little more probing, you learn that Bill Bentwick has a gambling problem. It is rumored that he has run up considerable debts with members of the underworld.

That last point tells you that Mr. Bentwick could be a desperate man. And a desperate man who has a large debt to repay could be roped into a crazy scheme —like the kidnapping of a rock-and-roll star.

Since Bentwick fits the description of the "electrician" seen in the high-school auditorium, you've got an important decision to make.

If you decide to take your information right to Lieutenant Trapp, turn to page 107.

If you decide to question Bentwick first, turn to page 110.